THIS BLOOMSBURY BOOK

BELONGS TO

....

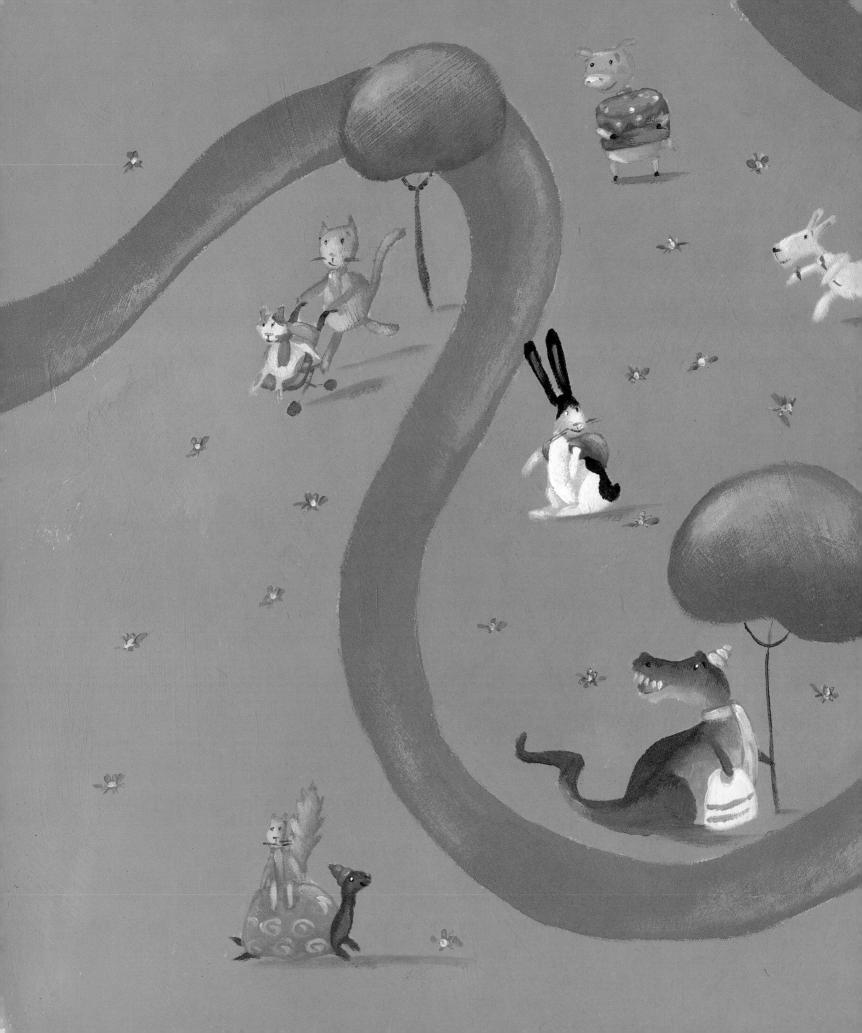

For Harry Sellen, with love — SR
To my dear friend Nick — JN

BLOOMSBURY
CHILDREN'S
BOOKS

First published in Great Britain in 2000 by Bloomsbury Publishing Plc,
36 Soho Square, London, W1D 3QY
This paperback edition first published in 2001

Text copyright © Shen Roddie 2000
Illustrations copyright © Jill Newton 2000

A CIP catalogue record of this book is available from the British Library

ISBN 0 7475 5028 X
9780747550280

Printed in China by South China Printing Co.

10 9 8 7 6

All papers used by Bloomsbury Publishing are natural, recyclable products made
from wood grown in well-managed forests. The manufacturing processes conform to
the environmental regulations of the country of origin.

Please Don't Chat
to the
Bus Driver

Shen Roddie and Jill Newton

BLOOMSBURY
CHILDREN'S
BOOKS

Here comes the bus! Up you go, Pig.

But please don't chat to the Bus Driver.
"I won't," said Pig.

But she did!

And the bus missed a stop!

Here comes the bus that missed a stop.
Up you go, Croc.

But please don't chat to the Bus Driver!
"I won't," said Croc.

But he did!
And the bus hit a tree!

Here comes the battered bus that missed a
stop. Up you go, Rabbit! But please don't
chat to the Bus Driver!
"I won't," said Rabbit.

But he did!
And the Bus Driver fell fast asleep!

Here comes the late, battered bus that missed a stop. Up you go, Fox.

But please don't chat to the Bus Driver!
"I won't," said Fox.

But he did!

And the Bus Driver fell on his horn, laughing! Honk, Honk blared the horn!

Here comes the noisy, late, battered bus that missed a stop. Up you go, Hen.

But please don't chat to the Bus Driver!
"I won't," said Hen.

But she did!
And the dizzy Bus Driver spun
round and round the roundabout!

Here comes the spinning, noisy, late,
battered bus that missed a stop.
Up you go, Cow.

But please don't chat to the Bus Driver!
"I won't," said Cow.

But she did!
And the bus went the wrong way!

Here comes the lost, spinning, noisy, late, battered bus that missed a stop.
Up you go, Frog!

But please don't chat to the Bus Driver!
"I won't," said Frog.

But he did! And the bus shot over
a hump and lost a wheel!

The limping, lost, spinning, noisy, late, battered bus that missed a stop, stopped!

"All out!" shouted the Bus Driver. Everybody scrambled out.

Here comes the next bus. Up you go, everyone! And remember —

don't chat to the Bus Driver!

"We won't," said Pig, Croc, Rabbit,
Fox, Hen, Cow and Frog.

But they did!

Acclaim for this book